The Adventures of Sam Pig

The Christmas Box

Alison Uttley

Illustrated by Graham Percy

faber and faber

LONDON · BOSTON

First published in 1939
by Faber and Faber Limited
3 Queen Square London WC1N 3AU
This edition first published in 1988

Printed in Great Britain by
W. S. Cowell Ltd Ipswich

Text © The Alison Uttley
Literary Property Trust, 1939, 1988
Illustrations © Graham Percy, 1988

British Library Cataloguing in Publication Data

Uttley, Alison
The Christmas box. –
(The Adventures of Sam Pig).
I. Title   II. Percy, Graham   III. Series
823′.912[J]   PZ7

ISBN 0–571–15164–7

The Christmas Box

It was December, and every morning when Sam Pig awoke he thought about Christmas Day. He looked at the snow, and he shivered a little as he pulled on his little trousers and ran downstairs. But the kitchen was warm and bright and a big fire burned in the hearth. Tom cooked the porridge and Ann set the table with spoons and plates, and Sam ran out to sweep the path or to find a log for the fire.

After breakfast Sam fed the birds. They came flying down from the woods, hundreds of them, fluttering and crying and stamping their tiny feet, and flapping their slender wings. The big birds – the green woodpeckers, the blue spangled jays, the dusky rooks and the speckled thrushes – ate from large earthen dishes and stone troughs which Sam filled with scraps. They were always so hungry that the little birds got no chance, so Sam had a special breakfast table for robins and tom-tits, for wrens and chaffinches. On a long flat stone were ranged rows of little polished bowls filled with crumbs and savouries.

The bowls were walnut shells, and every bird had its own tiny brown nutshell. Sam got the shells from the big walnut tree in the corner of the farmer's croft. When autumn came the nuts fell to the ground, and Sam carried them home in a sack. The walnuts were made into nut-meal, but the shells were kept for the smallest birds.

After the bird-feeding Sam went out on his sledge. Sometimes Bill and Tom and Ann rode with him. Badger had made the sledge, but he never rode on it himself. He was too old and dignified, but he enjoyed watching the four pigs career down the field and roll in a heap at the bottom.

'Good old Badger,' thought Sam. 'I will give him a nice Christmas present this year. I'll make him something to take back to his house in the woods when he goes for his winter sleep.'

Badger, of course, never retired before Christmas, but when the festival was over he disappeared for three months and left the little family alone.

That was as far as Sam got. Ann was busy knitting a muffler for Badger. It was made of black and white sheep's wool, striped to match

Badger's striped head. Bill the gardener was tending a blue hyacinth which he kept hidden in the woodshed. Tom the cook had made a cake for Brock. It was stuffed with currants and cherries and almonds as well as many other things like honeycomb and ants' eggs. Only young Sam had nothing at all.

There was plenty of time to make a present, he told himself carelessly, and he swept up the snow from the path and collected the small birds' walnut shells.

'Christmas is coming,' said a robin brightly. 'Have you got your Christmas cards ready, Sam?'

'Christmas cards?' said Sam. 'What's that?'

'You don't know what a Christmas card is?

Why, I'm part of a Christmas card! You won't have a good Christmas without a few cards, Sam.'

Sam went back to the house, where Ann sat by the fire knitting Badger's muffler. She used a pair of holly-wood knitting needles which Sam had made. A pile of scarlet holly-berries lay in a bowl by her side and she knitted a berry into the wool for ornament here and there. The blackthorn knitting needles with their little white flowers were, of course, put away for the winter. She only used those to knit spring garments.

Sam sat down by her side and took up the ball of wool. He rubbed it on his cheek and hesitated, but Ann went on knitting. She wondered what he was going to say.

'Ann. Can I make a Christmas card for Badger?' he asked.

Ann pondered this for a time, and her little needles clicked in tune with her thoughts.

'Yes, I think you can,' said she at last. 'I had forgotten what a Christmas card was like. Now I remember. There is a paintbox in the kitchen drawer, very very old. It belonged to our grandmother. She used to collect colours from the flowers and she kept them in a box. Go and look for it, Sam.'

Sam went to the drawer and turned over the odd collection of things. There were cough lozenges and candle-ends, and bits of string, and a bunch of rusty keys, a piece of soap and a pencil, all stuck together with gum from the larch trees. Then, at the back of the drawer, buried under the dead leaves and dried moss, he found the little paintbox.

'Here it is! Oh Ann! How exciting,' cried Sam, and he carried it to the table.

'It's very dry and the paints all look the same colour,' said Ann, 'but with a good wash they'll be all right.'

'It's a very nice box of paints,' said Sam, and he

licked each paint carefully with his pointed
tongue.

'They taste delicious,' said he, smacking his
lips. 'The colours are all different underneath,
and the tastes are like the colours. Look, Ann!
Here's red, and here's green and here's blue, all
underneath this browny colour.'

He held out the box of licked paints which
were now gaily coloured.

'The red tastes of tomatoes and the green of
wood-sorrel and the blue of forget-me-nots,' said
Sam.

Badger was much interested in the paintbox
when he came in.

'You will want a paint-brush,' said he. 'You can't use the besom-brush, or the scrubbing-brush, or even your tooth-brush to paint a Christmas card, Sam.'

'Nor can he use the Fox's brush,' teased Bill.

Badger plucked a few hairs from his tail and bound them together.

'Here! A badger-brush will be excellent, Sam.'

'What shall I have to paint on?' asked Sam, as he sucked the little brush to a point and rubbed it on one of the paints.

That puzzled everybody. There was no paper at all. They looked high and low, but it wasn't till Tom was cooking the supper that they found the right thing. Tom cracked some eggs and threw the shells in the corner. Sam took one up and used the badger-brush upon it.

'This is what I will have,' he cried, and indeed it was perfect, so smooth and delicate. Bill cut the edges neatly and Sam practised his painting upon it, making curves and flourishes.

'That isn't like a Christmas card,' said Ann, leaning over his shoulder. 'A Christmas card must have a robin on it.'

'You must ask the robin to come and be painted tomorrow,' said Brock. 'He will know all about it. Robins have been painted on Christmas cards for many years.'

After the birds' breakfast the next day Sam asked the robin to come and have a picture made.

'I will sit here on this holly branch,' said the robin. 'Here is the snow, and here's the holly. I can hold a sprig of mistletoe in my beak if you like.'

So Sam fetched his little stool and sat in the snow with his paintbox and the badger-brush, and the robin perched on the holly branch, with a mistletoe sprig in its beak. It puffed out its scarlet breast and stared with unwinking brown eyes at Sam, and he licked his brush and dipped it in the red and blue and green, giving the robin a blue feather and a green wing.

'More eggshells,' called Sam, and he painted so fast and so brightly that the robin took one look and flew away in disgust.

'That's a bird of Paradise,' said he crossly.

Sam took his eggshells indoors and hid them in a hole in the wall, ready for Christmas Day.

'Have you a Christmas present for Badger?' asked Ann. 'I have nearly finished my scarf, and Tom's cake is made, and Bill's hyacinth is in bud. What have you made, Sam?'

'Nothing except the Christmas card,' confessed Sam. 'I've been thinking and thinking, but I can't find anything. If I could knit a pair of stockings, or grow a cabbage, or make a pasty, I should know what to give him, but I can't do nothing.'

'Anything,' corrected Ann.

'Nothing,' said Sam. 'I can play my fiddle – '

'And fall in the river and steal a few apples and get lost and catch the wind – ' laughed Ann. 'Never mind. You shall share my scarf if you like, Sam, for you helped to find the sheep's wool and you got the holly-berries for me.'

Sam shook his head. 'No. I won't share. I'll do something myself.'

He went out to the woods, trudging through the snow, looking for Christmas presents. In the holly trees were scarlet clusters of berries, and the glossy ivy was adorned with black beads. The rest of the trees, except the yews and fir trees, were bare, and they stood with boughs uplifted, and their trunks faintly smudged with snow. There wasn't a Christmas present anywhere among them. The willows, from which Badger had made the boat, were smooth and ruddy, with never a parcel or packet or treasure among them.

Then something waved in a thorn bush, something fluttered like a white flag, and Sam ran forward. The wind was rising and it made a curious moan and a whistle as it ruffled Sam's ears and made them ache. He stretched up to the little flag and found it was a feather. A feather! Sam had a thought! Perhaps the wind blew it to him, but there it was, a feather!

'I'll make him a feather bed, and when he goes to his castle deep in the woods he will take it with him to lie on. Poor old Badger, sleeping alone on the hard ground. Yes, I'll make him a feather bed.'

When the birds came for their breakfast the next morning Sam spoke to them about it.

'Can you spare a feather or two? I want to make a feather bed for old Badger's Christmas present,' he told them.

The birds shook their wings and dropped each a loose feather; they brushed and combed themselves and tossed little feathers to the ground. They passed the word round among the tree families, and other birds came flying with little feathers in their beaks for Sam Pig. A flock of starlings left a heap of glistening shot silk, and the rooks came cawing from the bare elms with sleek black quills. The chattering magpies brought their black and white feathers, which Sam thought were like Badger's head. The jays came with their bright blue jewels, and the robins with scarlet wisps from their breasts. A crowd of tits gave him their own soft little many-coloured feathers, and even the wood pigeons left grey feathers for Sam. He had so many the air was clouded with feathers so that it seemed to be snowing again.

He gathered them up and filled his sack, and even then he had some over. He put the beautiful tiny feathers in his pocket, the red scraps from the robins, the blue petals of feathers from the tits, the yellow atoms from the goldfinches and the emerald-blue gems from the kingfisher. These he wove into a basket as small as a nutshell, for Sister Ann, and inside he put some mistletoe pearls. Ann would like this, he knew.

On Christmas Day Sam came downstairs to the kitchen, calling 'A merry Christmas' to everybody. He didn't hang up his stocking, of course, because he had no stockings, and he didn't expect any presents either. Badger was the one who got the presents, old Badger who was the friend and guardian of the four pigs. It was at Christmas time they made their gifts to thank him for his care. So all the little pigs came hurrying downstairs with their presents for him.

There stood Badger, waiting for them, with a twinkle in his eye. Ann gave him the black and white muffler with its little scarlet berries interwoven.

'Here's a muffler for cold days in the forest, Brock,' said she.

'Just the thing for nights when I go hunting,' said Brock, nodding his head and wrapping the muffler round his neck.

Then Bill gave him the little blue hyacinth growing in a pot.

'Here's a flower for you, Brock, which I've reared myself.'

'Thank you, Bill. It's the flower I love,' said Brock and he sniffed the sweet scent.

Then Tom came forward with the cake, which was prickly with almonds and seeds from many a plant.

'Here's a cake, Brock, and it's got so many things inside it, I've lost count of them, but there's some honeycomb and eggs.'

'Ah! You know how I like a slice of cake,' cried Brock, taking the great round cake which was heavy as lead.

Then little Sam came, with the feather bed on his back. He had embroidered it with the letter B made of the black and white magpie feathers.

'Sam! Sam!' everybody cried. 'And you kept it secret! That's what you were doing every morning when the birds came for their breakfast! We thought there seemed to be a lot of feathers on the ground!'

Badger lay down on the little bed and pretended to snore. He was delighted with the warm comfortable present from little Sam Pig.

'Never mind the weather but sleep upon a feather,' said he. 'I shall sleep like a top through the fiercest gale when I lie on this little bed.'

They had breakfast, with a lashing of treacle on their porridge from the tin which Ann had kept for festivals. Then Sam hurried out to feed the birds and to thank them again for their share in Badger's Christmas. He carried a basket full of walnut shells stuffed with scraps, and he found hosts of birds hopping about waiting for him.

But when he stepped into the garden he gave a cry of surprise, for in the flower bed grew a strange little tree.

'Look! Look!' he called. 'Ann! Bill! Tom! Badger! Come and look! It wasn't growing there last night. Where has it come from? And look at the funny fruit hanging on it! What is it?'

They followed him out and stared in astonishment at the small fir tree, all hung with pretty things. There were sugar pigs with pink noses and curly tails of string; and sugar watches with linked chains of white sugar, and chocolate mice. There were rosy apples and golden oranges, and among the sweet dainties were glittering icicles and hoar-frost crystals.

'Where has it come from? How did it grow here?' they asked, and they turned to Badger. 'Is it a magic?' they asked. 'Will it disappear? Is it really real?'

'It's solid enough, for the tree has come from the woods, but the other things will disappear fast enough, I warrant, when you four get near them.'

'But where did you find such strange and lovely things?' persisted Ann, staring up with her little blue eyes. 'Where? Where? From Fairyland, Badger?'

'I went to the Christmas fair in the town. I walked up to a market stall and bought them with a silver penny I had by me,' said Brock.

'But did nobody say anything to you?' asked Sam. 'How did you escape?'

'They were all so busy they didn't notice a little brown man who walked among them. They didn't bother about me on Christmas Eve. Miracles happen on Christmas Eve, and perhaps I was one of them. Also I carried the Leprechaun's shoe in my hand and maybe that helped me.'

Then Sam Pig brought the little feather basket and hung it among the icicles for his sister Ann. She was enchanted by it, and strung the mistletoe pearls round her neck.

'But where are your Christmas cards, Sam?' she asked suddenly. 'This is the time to give them.'

'I sat on them, Ann,' confessed Sam. 'I put them on a chair and sat down on them.'

'Crushed Christmas cards,' murmured Tom the cook. 'They will do very well to give an extra flavour to the soup. Those reds and blues and greens will make the soup taste extra good, I'm sure.'

It was true. The Christmas soup with the Christmas card flavour was the nicest anyone had ever tasted, and not a drop was left.

As for the Christmas tree, everybody shared it, for the birds flew down to its branches and sang a Christmas carol in thanks for their breakfasts, and Sam sat underneath and sang another carol in thanks for their feathers.

So it was a very happy Christmas all round.